Poké Rap

I want to be the very best there ever was
To beat all the rest, yeah, that's my cause

Catch 'em, Catch 'em, Gotta catch 'em all

Pokémon I'll search across the land
Look far and wide
Release from my hand
The power that's inside

Catch 'em, Catch 'em, Gotta catch 'em all
Pokémon!

Gotta catch 'em all, Gotta catch 'em all
Gotta catch 'em all, Gotta catch 'em all

At least one hundred and fifty or more to see
To be a Pokémon Master is my destiny

Catch 'em, Catch 'em, Gotta catch 'em all
Gotta catch 'em all, Pokémon! (repeat three times)

Can YOU Rap all 150?

**Here's the next 32.
Check out book #12**
Scyther, Heart of a Champion
for more of the Poké Rap.

Zubat, Primeape, Meowth, Onix,
Geodude, Rapidash, Magneton, Snorlax,
Gengar, Tangela, Goldeen, Spearow,
Weezing, Seel, Gyarados, Slowbro.

Kabuto, Persian, Paras, Horsea,
Raticate, Magnemite, Kadabra, Weepinbell,
Ditto, Cloyster, Caterpie, Sandshrew,
Bulbasaur, Charmander, Golem, Pikachu.

Words and Music by Tamara Loeffler and John Siegler
Copyright © 1999 Pikachu Music (BMI)
Worldwide rights for Pikachu Music administered by Cherry River Music Co. (BMI)
All Rights Reserved   Used by Permission

There are more books
about Pokémon.

collect them all!

POKéMON™

The Four-star Challenge

Adapted by Howard Dewin

SCHOLASTIC INC.
New York   Toronto   London   Auckland   Sydney
Mexico City   New Delhi   Hong Kong

ISBN 0-439-16944-5

12 11 10 9 8 7 6 5 4 3   0 1 2 3 4 5/0

Printed in the U.S.A.
First Scholastic printing, August 2000

Full Speed Ahead!

"Go, Lapras!" Ash Ketchum shouted to his Water Pokémon. The big blue creature sped across the sparkling ocean waters that surrounded the Orange Islands.

Ash and his friends rode atop Lapras's sturdy, round back. His longtime friend, Misty, held her baby Pokémon, Togepi. His new friend, Tracey, drew in a sketchbook. And Pikachu, Ash's Electric Pokémon, smiled and enjoyed the ride.

"I think Lapras is having fun!" said Misty. Her orange hair blew in the ocean wind. She gave Togepi an affectionate squeeze. "And I should know! It *is* a Water Pokémon, after all."

Misty loved Water Pokémon. Even Ash had to admit, she knew more about them than anyone else he'd met.

"What's not to like?" Ash replied as he felt the warm tropical breeze on his face. "Being a Pokémon trainer is a great life!"

Sometimes he couldn't believe how far he'd come since his tenth birthday. That's when he left his home in Pallet Town and began his journey as a Pokémon trainer. He'd met a lot of people and had many adventures. But most important, he'd captured a lot of Pokémon since then.

"Pika-a-a-a!"

Pikachu's cry snapped Ash out of his daydream. The little yellow Pokémon was flying through the air, thrown off balance by a surprise wave. Ash dove after Pikachu, holding onto Lapras with his legs. He caught Pikachu just before it hit the water.

"That was a close one," he said.

"Pika," agreed Pikachu, its eyes still wide with surprise.

"We're not in a hurry, Lapras. You don't have to rush," said Misty.

"That's true," said Ash, "although I wouldn't mind getting something to eat."

"I'm kind of hungry, too," Misty agreed.

"Pikachu!" added Pikachu.

"Well, we're not that far from Mikan Island," said Tracey, a Pokémon watcher. "I'm sure we can get some food there. And — there's an Orange League Gym on the island."

"An Orange League Gym?!" Ash sat up, suddenly forgetting his hunger.

He came to the Orange Islands on an errand for his hometown mentor, Professor Oak, the famous Pokémon expert. The Professor wanted Ash, Misty, and their friend, Brock, to pick up a mysterious Poké Ball called the GS Ball from his old friend, Professor Ivy. Ash picked up the GS Ball, but he lost a friend. Brock decided to stay and help Professor Ivy.

Ash missed Brock but he soon found another friend, Tracey, and a new Pokémon, Lapras. And then he heard about the Orange League.

"I guess this is it, huh, Ash?" Misty said, knocking him with her elbow. "The beginning of a whole new challenge!"

Ash knew she was teasing him but he didn't care. He'd done pretty well in the Pokémon League back home. He couldn't wait to win the Orange League's four badges and then compete for the championship trophy in their league tournament. Misty could tease all she wanted!

"You just wait and see! I'm gonna be the greatest Pokémon trainer the Orange

Islands have ever seen!"
Ash said.

"*Pika pika!*" Pikachu
squeaked in agreement.

"See? Pikachu knows
I'm right!" Ash said.
"We're going to challenge
every Gym Leader on
these islands!"

Misty laughed and shook her head. "Too
bad you don't have any confidence, Ash
Ketchum."

Ash smiled at Pikachu. How could he not
feel confident? He and Pikachu made a
great team.

"Full speed ahead!" Tracey shouted.
"Next stop, Mikan Island!"

2

Water Pokémon Challenge

"Look!" cried Ash, "There it is!"

"Mikan Island," said Tracey.

Ash and his friends climbed down off Lapras's back onto the white sandy beach. It was a lush green tropical island and Ash couldn't wait to explore.

"Good work, Lapras," Ash said. "Return!" He held out a Poké Ball and with a puff of light, Lapras disappeared into the little red-and-white ball. Ash hooked it securely on his belt alongside his other Poké Balls. Only Pikachu traveled outside its Poké Ball because it absolutely hated to be inside one.

"They say Mikan's Gym Leader is one of the toughest trainers in the Orange Crew," said Tracey, already starting his next sketch.

"Wow!" exclaimed Ash. "A match with one of the toughest trainers in the Orange League! Now I really can't wait! Come on, let's go!"

"Nobody loves a Pokémon challenge more than Ash," Misty said, running to keep up.

"Kachu!" Pikachu was on Ash's heels, happy and excited to help him win his first Orange Islands badge.

They hiked through the jungle until a red-domed building appeared.

"There it is!" announced Tracey.

"All right!" shouted Ash, his pace quickening.

Suddenly, a young boy jumped out from behind a tree. "What are you doing here?" he asked accusingly.

"I'm a Pokémon trainer," Ash explained. "I'm looking for a gym battle."

The boy laughed. "You don't look like a Pokémon trainer."

"Oh, yeah?" snapped Ash. "I was good enough to compete in the Indigo League."

"Ha! The Orange League's way tougher than that!"

"Are you making trouble again?" a woman's voice came from behind the boy.

Ash, Misty, and Tracey looked up and saw a tall, young woman.

"No," the boy protested. "I just saw this guy sneaking around —"

"I was not sneaking," Ash demanded, "I've come to challenge the Gym Leader!"

"Is that so?" the woman asked. She smiled at Ash. "Well, I'm the Mikan Gym Leader and I accept your challenge."

Ash gasped. Pikachu stared with wide eyes.

"I'm Cissy, and this is my brother," she said. "Since you're just a little squirt, let's use Water Pokémon." She started to walk toward the gym.

"Hey! Who are you calling 'squirt'?!" Ash shouted as he ran to catch up.

The inside of the gym felt huge and empty to Ash. "Okay," he said, "how many Pokémon do you want to use?"

"That's not the way we do things around here," Cissy said. "In the Orange Island Gyms, we do a lot more than just have our Pokémon battle each other."

"What's that supposed to mean?" Ash asked.

"You'll see," said Cissy. "We'll decide the match with two challenges." She turned to her kid brother. "Hit it!"

"Right!" the boy said. He punched buttons on a remote control in his hands. Suddenly, everything was moving. Wall panels slid back and Ash saw a line of old tin cans lined up on a ledge. Then, part of the floor started to move.

"Yikes!" exclaimed Misty.

In the middle of the gym, a slide-away floor revealed a full-size swimming pool.

"Wow," Ash said. He was impressed but tried to hide it. "So what are the tin cans for?"

Cissy didn't stop to explain. She already had a Poké Ball in her hand. She hurled it forward, shouting, "Seadra! I choose you!"

From out of the Poké Ball came a blue Pokémon that looked like a seahorse. Its tail curled around in a coil and its mouth was like a long nozzle. It dove into the pool.

"What *is* that?" Ash asked under his breath.

He grabbed his Pokédex, a handheld device that stored a lot of information about Pokémon.

"Seadra," said the electronic voice o er, the Pokédex, "a Dragon Pokémon. The evolved form of Horsea. It is known for its horrible disposition but possesses both strength and speed."

"We'll start with a Water Gun Challenge," Cissy announced. "Pick whatever Pokémon has the best Water Gun Attack. In my gym, the Pokémon compete like athletes do, using their skills head-to-head, one-on-one."

Ash glanced at Pikachu, a little worried. The Orange League was really different.

Ash tried to appear confident, "Squirtle! I choose you!"

He hurled a Poké Ball and a small turtle-like Pokémon appeared. Squirtle looked tough and ready for battle.

"Squirtle," he whispered, "this isn't like any battle before. I'm counting on you."

"*Squirtle,*" replied the Water Pokémon.

"I hope your Squirtle's a good loser!" Cissy laughed and turned to Seadra. "Water Gun now!"

Seadra leaped into the air, spitting furious shots of water from its snout. *Bing! Bang! Ping! Pong!* Faster than lightning, Seadra shot and hit every one of the tin cans off the ledge.

Tracey started sketching wildly. "That's impressive!"

"I don't know if Squirtle can match that," Misty said quietly.

Ash didn't hesitate.

"Okay, Squirtle. Ready, aim, fire!" Ash shouted.

Squirtle jumped into the air and spit out one blast of water after another. *Bam! Slam! Crash! Wham!* Every one of the cans went flying off the ledge!

"All right!" cheered Ash.

"Not bad," Cissy muttered. "Let's try moving targets."

"Here they come!" shouted her brother. He pushed more buttons on his remote control.

Whizzz! A flying disk sailed over Ash's head.

"Fire!" shouted Cissy. Seadra sailed up into the air and sent out a speeding column of water from its nozzlelike mouth. It hit the disk dead center. The target exploded into pieces.

"Triple!" Cissy shouted.

Three more disks sailed into the air. Seadra spit three fast spouts of water at the targets. *Bang! Bang! Bang!* All three disks shattered in midair.

"Whoa . . . " Ash was amazed. "Okay, Squirtle — give it your best shot!"

One disk flew into the air. *Bang!* Squirtle didn't miss a beat.

"Good work!" Ash shouted. "Now go for three."

Bang! Bang! Bang! Squirtle was unstoppable!

"Next is a quick-draw contest," Cissy said. "Whoever hits the disk first, wins."

The gym went silent. Everyone looked up at the ceiling and waited for the disk to

appear. Tracey looked through binoculars, ready to call the winner.

"Go!" cried the boy. A disk flew across the gym. Seadra and Squirtle both leaped out of the water. They each aimed powerful shots of water at the target. One enormous bang rang out as the disk exploded. It was impossible to tell which Pokémon had hit it first. Everyone looked at Tracey.

"They hit at the same time," he announced. "It's a draw!"

"Then," Cissy said slowly. "The outcome is going to depend on the Pokémon Wave Ride."

Ash looked at Cissy, hoping she would explain. But she was already walking out the door, headed down to the beach.

"Wave Ride?" Ash asked.

Ash didn't know what to expect. This was turning out to be his toughest match yet!

3

The Coral-Eye Badge

"What's wave riding?" Ash asked. He stood on the beach and stared at the water.

"The Pokémon just have to swim around that flag out there," Cissy said.

Ash squinted to see the distant marker.

"The first to come back wins!" Cissy looked very confident.

"This'll be easy!" Ash crowed.

"Blastoise! I choose you." Cissy called forth the huge Pokémon. The evolved form of Squirtle and Wartortle, Blastoise looked like a giant turtle with two water cannons coming out of its shell.

"I know the way to beat Blastoise," Ash whispered to Tracey. "Lapras! I choose you!" he called.

In a swirl of white mist, Lapras came flying out of its Poké Ball. It looked gentle and sweet next to Blastoise. But Ash knew it was a really strong swimmer.

"Let's get going!" Cissy commanded.

Her brother held the starting gun in the air. Ash stood tensely by Lapras, ready to command its every move. Blastoise stood rock solid, waiting for the sound of the gun.

Suddenly, a giant submarine shaped like a Magikarp exploded to the surface of the water. Standing on top of the sub were a teenage girl, a teenage boy, and a catlike Pokémon.

It was Jessie, James, and Meowth, a trio of Pokémon thieves known as Team Rocket.

"Prepare for tropical trouble!" shouted red-haired Jessie.

"Make it desert-island double!" James joined in.

"To protect the world from devastation —"

Ash and Misty shook their heads. They were tired of hearing Team Rocket's nasty chant.

"It's the same thing every time," sighed Ash.

"Are these friends of yours?" Cissy asked.

"Hardly!" Misty sneered.

"We want that Pikachu and we want it now!" Jessie shouted.

"You'll never get Pikachu!" Ash shouted back.

"Weezing, go!" James threw a Poké Ball up into the sky and a Pokémon belching smoke came pouring out. A black haze filled the air and Ash couldn't breathe. Everyone on the beach gasped for air.

"Fire the net!" Jessie shouted. Suddenly, a gigantic net fell inches from Ash's face. He dove to protect Pikachu but the net missed his Pokémon. Instead, it landed on Blastoise. Team Rocket jumped into their submarine.

"Blastoise!" Ash yelled.

The submarine pulled Blastoise through the water. Ash looked at Cissy, who stood calmly watching.

"We have to save Blastoise!" Ash cried.

"Blastoise can handle those three," she said in a steady voice.

Ash looked out to sea. Blastoise was sinking beneath the water, pulled down by the weight of the sub. Then it was gone!

Ash, Misty, Tracey, and Pikachu stared in shock, hoping to see the giant Pokémon reappear. But there was nothing.

"Are you sure we shouldn't try to do something?" Misty asked.

"I'm sure," said Cissy.

At that very moment, the waters exploded. Blastoise came hurling up out of the sea, pulling the submarine and Team Rocket with it. The net ripped away as if it were made of paper. Blastoise was free!

"I guess you were right!" Ash exclaimed.

"Told you!" Cissy smiled.

"Those guys never learn," Ash said, shaking his head. "Pikachu, go!"

Pikachu dashed to the water's edge. It

turned its lightning bolt tail to the water and dipped it into the tide. *Ccrraaaccckk!* Electricity shot across the water's surface and lit up Team Rocket like a Christmas tree! Then Blastoise fired off a round of cannon blasts. The blasts blew the electrified team sky-high. They were nowhere to be seen.

"Looks like Team Rocket blasted off again!" cheered Misty.

Cissy frowned impatiently. "Let's start this race!" she demanded.

"Okay!" said Ash, "Get out there and do your best, Lapras!"

Cissy climbed on top of Blastoise. "Well, get on already, Ash!"

"On?"

Cissy grinned. "The trainer stands on the Pokémon in the Wave Ride. If you fall off, you lose."

Ash stared at her in disbelief. Standing on the Pokémon? He hadn't realized he was supposed to ride on Lapras.

Ash took a deep breath and climbed on Lapras's back.

Bang! The starting gun fired.

Ash almost immediately lost his balance, but he held himself steady.

"Try to move to the inside, Lapras!" Ash shouted. He knew the inside track was the best place to be in a race. If he could get it, he'd round the marker faster.

"Don't let them, Blastoise!" Ash could hear Cissy shout. Suddenly, Lapras shook as Blastoise crashed into its side.

"Try for the inside again!" Ash shouted to his Pokémon. This time, Lapras smashed into Blastoise.

"You've got guts, squirt! But we've got strength!" Cissy's voice sailed over the crashing waves, "Bash 'em, Blastoise!"

The Pokémon came at Lapras from the side with a fury. The power of the impact threw Ash off his feet and into the air.

"Ash is falling!" screamed Misty.

But Lapras swooped down with its big neck and snatched Ash out of midair.

"Nice catch, Lapras!" Ash said.

Cissy was rounding the marker. Ash had to catch up before she got too far ahead. He and Lapras rounded the marker and sped up behind Cissy.

"You're better than I thought you'd be!" she shouted.

"So are you!" Ash shouted back. They were neck and neck.

"Look out!" Misty's scream cut through the air.

"Cis-sy!" her kid brother shouted, panicked.

Cissy and Ash turned to see a huge tidal wave rising behind them. Ash knew it would crush them in a matter of seconds. He braced for the impact.

Then Lapras turned to face the enormous wave. It opened its mouth and sent out a glowing orb of light. The orb hit the water and the water froze instantly. Ash was safe!

"Ice Beam! Nice work, Lapras," Ash said.

But the water behind Cissy didn't freeze fast enough. It came crashing down on her. She and Blastoise hurled through the air.

"Ciisss-sssyyy!" Her brother was terrified.

Blastoise crashed down into the waves seconds before Cissy. Its large shell rose up out of the water just in time for Cissy to land on it.

"You saved me, Blastoise!" she said. Blastoise didn't miss a beat. It raced up next to Lapras and toward the finish line.

"See ya at the finish line!" Cissy yelled to Ash as she pulled farther ahead.

"You gave me an idea, Lapras," Ash told the Pokémon. "Aim an Ice Beam straight to the shore!"

Lapras opened its mouth and shot another golden orb across the water to the beach. A frozen path rose up from the water.

"Now get on top of the ice, Lapras!" Ash commanded.

Lapras leaped onto the ice. They took off at an amazing speed. Gliding on the ice was ten times faster than swimming. Ash and Lapras sailed closer and closer to Cissy. Finally, they passed her! Skating at top speed, Ash and Lapras slid straight across

the finish line and didn't slow down until they crashed onto the beach!

Pikachu jumped into Ash's arms.

"I guess we won it," Ash said proudly.

Cissy jumped off Blastoise. "Great race, Ash," she said. "Pretty smart, using Lapras's Ice Beam."

"Yeah," chimed in her brother, "that was really cool."

"I think you're gonna do pretty well in the Orange League." Cissy smiled at him.

Ash beamed. He felt great.

Cissy held out her hand. She held a pink coral shell with a sapphire blue stone in the middle.

"This is the Coral-Eye Badge of the Mikan Gym," Cissy said. "It's proof that you've won your match."

"It looks like a shell," Ash said.

"All the Orange League badges are shells," Cissy said.

Ash took the badge from Cissy. He let out a cheer and shouted triumphantly, "I won the Coral-Eye Badge!"

4

Sky-high Gym

"It feels like we've been out on the ocean for days!" Ash moaned. Riding on Lapras was fun, but he wanted to get to his next battle.

"We should see Navel Island any time now," Tracey said, scanning the horizon.

"Pika!" Pikachu jumped up and down. Then it pointed. In the distance, partly covered in clouds, a volcano-like mountain rose up from the ocean.

"There it is," Tracey said. "Navel Island, home of the Sea Ruby badge."

"The Sea Ruby Badge," Ash said dreamily. He could already picture it being handed to him. "Step on it, Lapras!"

Soon they pulled up onto the beach. Ash spotted a small village in the distance.

"Let's see if anyone's there," he said.

They walked along the beach. Then a voice came out of nowhere.

"I bet you guys are looking for a gym battle!"

Ash spun around. A tall, athletic young man stood on the beach. He smiled at them.

"Uh . . . yeah," said Ash.

"Well, you came to the right place! Nice to meet you. I'm Dan."

"Hi. I'm Ash," Ash replied. He shook Dan's hand. "And these are my friends, Pikachu, Tracey, and Misty."

"Misty?" Dan repeated when Ash introduced her.

"Yeah," she said, shyer than usual.

"That's a very pretty name," Dan said. Misty blushed a little.

"Can you just take us to the gym?" Ash asked anxiously.

"My pleasure," Dan answered. "Follow me."

"Who is he?" Tracey asked as they followed Dan down a long, stone path.

"Beats me." Ash shrugged his shoulders. "He must be here to challenge the Gym Leader, too."

They hiked on for awhile. Then Ash caught sight of an enormous stone wall. It looked like it was built directly at the base of the huge mountain that they'd seen earlier.

"What's that?" Ash asked, pointing up ahead.

"That's the entrance to the gym," Dan told him.

They walked through two giant steel doors. Standing on the other side of the wall, Ash found himself looking straight up the biggest, steepest mountain he'd ever seen.

"I don't get it," he said softly. "Where's the gym?"

Misty pointed to a cable car that ran all the way to the top of the mountain. "I guess we have to take that cable car to the top. Maybe the gym is up there."

Tracey was already reading a nearby sign that said WELCOME, POKÉMON TRAINERS. Then he stopped and gave Ash a funny look.

"What?" Ash was getting annoyed.

Tracey continued to read. "All challengers to the Navel Gym must first climb to the top of the mountain. Trainers must climb using their power alone. Any trainer who uses a Pokémon will be disqualified."

Ash's eyebrows furrowed as he tried to understand what Tracey had just read.

"Climb?" he asked in disbelief.

Slowly, he turned his focus upward toward the mountain. A long, thin, winding path moved ever higher to the top of the mountain. At least he thought it did. The mountaintop was so far up that it was hidden in the clouds!

"It also says," Tracey continued, "that those who accompany challengers should use the cable car."

"Whew," Misty sighed in relief.

"So," Ash swallowed hard. "What you're saying is — I have to climb it . . . alone."

"Not completely," said Dan. "I'll be climbing too!"

5

Into the clouds

Ash stared up at the mountain. It didn't seem possible to climb such a steep slope, especially without the help of his Pokémon.

"Pika pi!" Pikachu clung to his shoulder, giving him a look of total confidence.

"You're right, Pikachu, I can do it. I can do it if I try," Ash said.

"Good luck, Ash!" Tracey shouted to him from the cable car. He and Misty were already headed to the top.

"Be careful, Dan!" Misty yelled out.

"Hey! What about me?" Ash yelled back.

"You be careful, too," Misty said.

Dan started up the mountain. Ash took a deep breath and followed.

"Pika pi!" Pikachu climbed ahead, calling back encouragement to Ash. They climbed and climbed until the mountain got so steep that Ash was clinging to its side, scaling it inch by inch. He made the mistake of looking down and suddenly he felt very dizzy. It was a straight drop down! There were already clouds swirling around him.

Ash closed his eyes and took a deep breath. One step at a time, he told himself as he reached out for the next little rock he could grip.

But that rock wasn't strong enough to hold him. Suddenly Ash was falling backward through the sky!

"Help!" he shouted. His arms and legs scrambled to find something to grab. Then he crashed against a rock ledge. He grabbed the ledge and clung with all his might.

Ash reached for a Poké Ball.

"Bulbasaur!" he choked out, " . . . use your vine . . . "

35

"Ash!" Dan shouted to him from above. "Don't do it!"

Ash remembered. If he used his Pokémon, he'd be disqualified.

He summoned up every bit of strength in his body and slowly crawled up onto the ledge. Then he began to climb, step by step, back up the mountain to where Pikachu waited. Finally, he and Pikachu caught up with Dan. They rested on a plateau big enough for the three of them. Ash was panting, exhausted and relieved.

"Thanks, Dan," he said, "I would have been disqualified without you."

"No problem," he said cheerfully. "Ready to finish our climb?" Dan asked.

Ash nodded and the three headed upward once again.

The steep mountain gave way to a more gradual incline but now there was snow everywhere. Bitter cold wind lashed at Ash's skin. He buried his face in his collar.

"Pika . . . pika . . . aaaa —"

Ash spun around. Pikachu was face-down in the snow.

"Pikachu!" Ash cried. How could he have let his Pokémon get so tired? "Are you all right?"

Pikachu looked up at him, too frozen to speak. Ash ripped off his vest and quickly wrapped it around the Pokémon.

"This should help," Ash said. "Don't worry. I'll hold you close and you'll get warm. No mountain's going to beat us!"

"Pika." It looked up at Ash with great admiration.

Ash suddenly stopped feeling sorry for

himself. It was up to him to get them safely up the mountain. He picked up Pikachu and marched straight past Dan, a brand-new determination in his step.

"Ash!" He heard Tracey's voice before he saw him.

"Great job, you guys!" Misty was wrapped in a bright red blanket, waving at them as they reached the top.

"I told you we'd make it!" Ash said as if he'd never doubted it.

He stopped and looked around. It felt like they were standing at the top of the world with a beautiful blue sky and crisp clear air. But where was the gym?

"Congratulations, Ash!" Danny said, coming up from behind. "It was quite a test and you passed!"

"Huh? I passed?"

"I knew it!" Misty said, looking at Dan and smiling.

"Yeah," chimed in Tracey. "I figured it out when we got to the top and nobody else was here."

"What are you guys talking about?" Ash

stared at his friends, puzzled.

"Dan's not here to win a badge, Ash," Misty said. "He's the Gym Leader!"

Ash spun around and stared at Dan.

Dan grinned. "It's true! I'm the Navel Island Gym Leader. Are you ready for our match?"

Ash was stunned but he quickly recovered. "Of course I'm ready! Aren't we, Pikachu?"

"Pika!"

"Great!" Dan exclaimed. "We'll decide the winner in three rounds. If you can win two out of three, you'll get the Sea Ruby Badge."

Danny held out a beautiful white shell with a red stone in its middle. Inside the red stone was a green emerald-like gem.

"Wow," was all Ash could say.

"First," Dan announced, "the geyser!"

He stepped back and revealed one bare patch of ground surrounded by snow.

Suddenly two huge fountains of water erupted from that spot. They sprayed high up into the sky. Hot steam filled the air.

"Whoever can freeze this water first, wins," Dan explained.

Ash had to think quickly. How could he freeze boiling water? He was going to lose this match even before it started!

6

Charizard Gets Busy

"Nidoqueen! I choose you!" Dan shouted. He hurled a Poké Ball into the open sky. An incredibly strong-looking Pokémon appeared. Its body was covered with blue plates that looked like armor.

Ash stared at Nidoqueen and realized what he needed. "Ice Attacks!" he said under his breath. "Lapras! I choose you!"

Lapras stood next to Nidoqueen. Ash was sure it had the power to win.

"Ice Beam Attack!" Ash and Dan shouted at the same time.

Both Pokémon shot glowing orbs of ice-beam light toward the powerful geysers. The geysers were beginning to turn into clear crystals of ice from the bottom up.

Nidoqueen's beam seemed to race up the geyser.

Lapras's beam was strong, but it moved more slowly.

"Hang in there, Lapras!" Ash shouted. "You can do it!"

"Nidoqueen, full power now!" Dan commanded. Nidoqueen's beam moved even faster, almost to the top. Lapras's beam was barely halfway up the geyser.

"Lapras —!" Ash shouted, but it was too late.

Nidoqueen's geyser was frozen solid.

"Pika!" Pikachu was amazed. Finally, Lapras finished. Both geysers stood frozen in midair.

"Looks like I win the first round!" Dan stated.

"Good job, Lapras," Ash said. He knew Lapras had done its best.

Dan and his Pokémon now carefully lowered the frozen geysers to the ground.

"In the second round," Dan explained, "we'll compete in ice sculpting. The first one to carve an ice sled out of the frozen geyser — using only three Pokémon — wins."

Ash stared at the frozen columns of ice.

"So, Ash," Dan turned to him. "Do you know which three you want to use?"

Ash studied the ice slabs. "Yes, I know exactly which three!"

Misty looked at him, anxious to hear what he'd decided.

"Pikachu!"

Pikachu jumped to attention, happy for the challenge.

"Bulbasaur!"

A combination Grass-Poison Pokémon with a bulb on its back appeared. Misty and Tracey leaned in, waiting to hear Ash's third choice.

"Charizard!" he shouted. The Fire Pokémon stood in line with Pikachu and Bulbasaur. Charizard looked like a big dragon, and its personality was as fierce as its appearance.

"Not Charizard," Tracey and Misty moaned in unison.

"Yes, Charizard!" Ash said proudly. "It's got the fire power to carve ice."

"But it never does anything you ask!" Misty reminded him.

Ash ignored her. He was sure that — this time — Charizard would listen to him.

"I'm using Machoke, Scyther, and Nidoqueen," Dan said.

"Pika!"

"Bulba!" Ash's little Pokémon eyed the larger opponents nervously.

Charizard yawned.

"Let's go!" Dan shouted and the second round began.

Pikachu and Bulbasaur sprang into action. Pikachu sent one electrical blast after another toward the ice, chipping it away tiny piece by tiny piece. Bulbasaur's vines whipped around, slowly making dents in the rock-hard ice. Charizard lay on its side, yawning and ignoring the crowd.

"Charizard, come on!" Ash pleaded. "I can't win without you."

Dan's sled was already taking shape. Machoke carved the ice with swift karate chops. Scyther's sharp claws acted like saws, making big clean slices. Nidoqueen shaped the ice by pounding it with raw strength.

"Charizard! Just this once," Ash pulled the tail of the giant dragon, trying to move it to action. Charizard snorted, a tiny flame shooting from its nose. It yawned.

Misty hung her head. "That Pokémon never listens."

Dan's sled was starting to take on some detail. Pikachu and Bulbasaur worked feverishly, but they were far behind. Ash pulled and pulled on Charizard's tail but it wouldn't budge. It shot an annoyed look at Ash and closed its eyes. Then, without even standing up, Charizard turned its head in the direction of the column of ice and let out three roaring blasts of fire.

Pikachu and Bulbasaur were thrown into the snow from the fury of Charizard's flame. Everyone was silent. They couldn't believe what they saw. Ash's shapeless block of ice was now a perfectly carved ice sled!

"Yeah, Charizard!" Ash leaped into the air. "We did it!"

Tracey and Misty shouted in disbelief, "Way to go!"

"Well, I don't know how," Dan shook his head, "but you won the second round, Ash!"

"Yes!" Ash shouted, "Pikachu . . . Bulbasaur . . . Charizard! Thank you so much!"

Pikachu and Bulbasaur looked happily at Ash. Charizard snorted and went back to sleep.

"The third round," Danny said, "is a sled race. The first team to the beach wins."

Dan led them to a new location. Ash strained to see the beach from where they stood. They were on the edge of a clifflike drop-off. It was a very long, steep slope that fell all the way down to the ocean. Down

48

near the water was a red flag. Ash gave his Pokémon a confident nod.

"This will be fun!" Ash said as he slid into the sled. Pikachu, Squirtle, and Bulbasaur wedged themselves in behind him.

"We'll meet you at the bottom!" Tracey said. He and Misty ran to the cable car.

"It's all downhill from here, Ash!" Misty joked. She turned to Dan. "Good luck, Dan!"

Ash shot her a dirty look. He couldn't believe she would root for his opponent!

"Ready," said Dan, "GO!"

The two sleds hit top speed in a matter of seconds.

"Right . . . now left!" Dan coached his Pokémon as they steered the sled.

"Left . . . I mean . . . right!" Ash shouted. Bulbasaur used its vines as rudders. Faster and faster, everything was starting to blur as they *whooshed* along at incredible speed.

Even so, Dan's sled whizzed past them. Soon Ash couldn't even see his opponent. They were so far behind, Ash wasn't sure how they'd ever catch up.

Then, suddenly, Dan and his sled appeared. They had crashed!

"Are you okay?!" Ash shouted, screeching his sled to a halt.

"I think so," Dan said, a little shaky. "But that was no accident. Somebody dug that hole." He pointed to a ditch dug right in the middle of the course.

Ash didn't even have to look at the hole to know what had happened.

"Team Rocket!" he said furiously.

"Good guess!" Meowth screeched as it popped out from behind a snowbank.

"But wait until you see the real hole!" Jessie and James popped out next.

Meowth pushed a button on a remote control it held in its paw. Suddenly, the snow beneath Ash, Dan, and their Pokémon gave way. The whole crew fell twenty feet and crashed to the bottom of a snowy pit.

"I hate those guys," Ash muttered as he tried to pick himself up. Before he could even steady himself, a metal arm came shooting down from above. Its claw snatched Pikachu from behind.

"Pikachu!" Ash grabbed for his Pokémon, but it was too late. Pikachu was flying backward, up out of the hole. Team Rocket's giant hot air balloon sailed overhead. The metal arm was pulling Pikachu up to the balloon. Ash watched as Jessie reached out and grabbed Pikachu from the metal claw.

Ash could hear Jessie laughing. "Now we've got you!" she said. "But better than that — we've got your Pikachu!"

7

Geodude to the Rescue!

"Nice friends you've got," Dan said sarcastically. He climbed up the side of the hole behind Ash, who was using Bulbasaur's vines to pull himself out.

"They're not my friends. And they're not nice!" Ash shot back.

Once out, he scanned the skies. Team Rocket's balloon was floating farther and farther away. And Pikachu was on board.

"What am I gonna do?" Ash wailed, helpless.

He looked to Dan for help. Dan was

silent as he stared at the balloon. Suddenly, his face brightened.

"Geodude!" Dan shouted. "I choose you!"

Dan's Rock Pokémon appeared. Geodude looked like a big round rock with long arms.

Dan was already making a pile of snowballs.

"Rock Throw, Geodude!" Dan yelled.

Ash suddenly understood. "Squirtle, Bulbasaur," Ash cried, "start making snowballs!"

In no time at all, Geodude was hurling dozens of snowballs up at the balloon. Its

long arms looked like a windmill moving around and around, firing off an endless assault of snowball fire. Geodude never missed its mark! Ash could see the balloon sagging under the weight of the basket, now filled with snow.

Then Geodude fired off a huge ball that slammed into the middle of the balloon. It turned the basket nearly upside down. Pikachu came flying over the side. Ash swooped in and caught Pikachu as Team Rocket's balloon exploded, sending the evil trio blasting off toward the horizon.

"Wow, Dan! That was great! Thank you," Ash said. He hugged Pikachu.

"Pika!" Pikachu smiled, happy to be back with Ash.

"No problem," Dan said. "Are you ready to finish the race?"

"Ready when you are!" Ash exclaimed. He and his Pokémon jumped back onto their ice sled. "I have to win this and get the badge!"

"Ready . . . set . . . go!" Dan shouted.

Almost immediately, the course felt different. Ash looked down. The snow was disappearing, giving way to rock. Ash looked ahead just in time to see Dan expertly swerve to avoid a huge boulder right in the middle of the course.

"Bulbasaur," Ash screeched, "we're headed right for that rock!"

Bulbasaur used its vines, grabbing for anything it could that might help pull their sled in another direction. Bulbasaur finally got hold of a tree trunk and pulled the sled just to the left of the boulder. But the adjustment sent the sled careening off the cleared path and into the forest. They narrowly missed hitting trees and tree branches as the sled raced ever faster, out of control. The sled banged up and down as it sped over bumps in the terrain.

"Aaaaaaahhhhhh!" Ash shouted.

Suddenly there were no bumps. It was like the ground disappeared beneath them. Ash uncovered his eyes and looked down. The ground *had* disappeared! The last bump they'd hit had sent them flying up into the air. They were sailing through the sky!

Down on the beach, Tracey and Misty were watching Dan race toward the finish line with Ash nowhere in sight. Then the flying sled appeared.

"What is that?!" Misty cried, pointing up at the sky.

Ash was flying directly over Dan. Then the sled began to arc back down toward land. They were nearly to the beach. *Bam!* They landed just in front of Dan.

"Wow!" shouted Tracey, sketching quickly to capture Ash's amazing flight.

Ash sailed across the finish line and kept going at full speed.

"Hang on!" he cried. The sled sped straight into the water.

"He won!" Misty stuttered in disbelief.

"He beat me." Dan was amazed. He walked up to Ash who was sitting in the water, still dazed from the ride.

"That sure was a rough ride!" Ash said.

"You were great, Ash," Dan said. "You chose your Pokémon well and you won two out of three." Dan held out his hand and in it sat the Sea Ruby Badge. "It's yours, Ash."

Ash reached up and took the badge. He stared at it for a second and then sprang out of the water.

"I did it! I earned the Sea Ruby Badge!"

"That was great!" Tracey announced.

"Pika!" Pikachu jumped up into Ash's arms.

"Good luck with the rest of your journey," Dan said after the crew had quieted down. "I'm guessing you'll hit Trovita Island next. It's a tough challenge."

Ash looked at his new badge. "It may be tough," he said. "But after this, I can handle anything!"

8

The One and Only Prima

Ash and his friends headed for Trovita Island and the next Orange Islands badge. After a few days, they decided they needed to stop for a short rest.

"Mandarin Island might not have a badge, but it sure does have great food," said Ash between huge bites of sandwich. "Not to mention tons of trainers looking for battles!"

As usual, Ash hadn't rested for long. He'd had lots of practice battling trainers since arriving on the island. And he'd won every challenge! Ash felt great.

"I wonder what Tracey's up to?" Misty said, looking over the beach from their table at the outdoor restaurant.

"Mmm-mmmm-mmm," Ash said, his mouth stuffed with food. Then he swallowed. "Anyway, I just want to finish lunch so I can go beat some more trainers!"

"I'm sure," Misty said, rolling her eyes.

"I'm unstoppable!" he exclaimed.

"You guys!" Tracey yelled, running up to them. "You'll never guess who's here!"

He held up a flyer.

Attention Trainers!

Pokémon lecture and battle demonstration by the one and only Prima!

Misty's eyes grew wide. "Prima! She's here? I'm her biggest fan! Not only is she one of the best trainers but she uses Water Pokémon!"

"Wow!" said Ash. "Let's go! I want to challenge her myself!"

"You can't just challenge Prima," Misty said. "She's one of the greatest Pokémon trainers in the world."

"Is someone talking about me?" A soft, peaceful voice came from behind them. They swung around. Standing before them was Prima herself! Tall and elegant, she looked at them sweetly.

"P-P-Prima," Misty was tongue-tied.

"Is it really you?" Tracey wasn't much better.

Then they started firing off questions. "Can I have your autograph?" "Do you come here every year?" "How can I train my Pokémon better?" But it seemed like Prima didn't hear them. She walked up to Togepi and tickled it under the chin. Then, she stared out at the ocean and closed her eyes.

"The sun feels wonderful, doesn't it? Open your ears, listen to the wind," Prima said.

"Are you listening to us?" Ash asked, annoyed. "How about a Pokémon battle?"

Misty glared at him.

"Hey!" said Ash, "I've won every battle on this island. I might have a chance! So? How about it?"

"There's nothing like being in nature," was Prima's reply.

Ash stormed away. He'd prove how good he was. Just below the deck of the restaurant was a trainer ready for a battle.

"Hey, mister!" Ash shouted, flashing his badges, "how about a Pokémon battle?"

"I accept," the older boy replied. "How about two Pokémon each?"

"Deal! Squirtle, I choose you!" Ash cried as Squirtle flew out of its Poké Ball.

"Go, Persian!" shouted the boy. He sneered at Ash. "You can go first with your cute little Squirtle."

"I'll show you," Ash bragged. "Squirtle! Water Gun!"

Squirtle shot a blast of water through the air straight at the Persian, but the catlike Pokémon was fast. Squirtle's shot missed.

"Persian! Thunderbolt!"

Ash couldn't believe his ears. A Persian with Electric Attacks? Before he could react, Squirtle was thrown backward by the force of the electrical jolt.

"Keep going, Squirtle! Skull Bash!"

Squirtle pulled itself up and slammed into the Persian, knocking it unconscious.

"All right!" Ash cried.

"Tauros! I choose you!" The other trainer was already calling up a huge Pokémon that looked like a bull. It pawed at the ground.

"Tackle!" the trainer commanded.

Tauros charged at Squirtle and sent it

crashing into the ground. This time Squirtle couldn't recover.

"Return, Squirtle!" Ash cried. "Charizard, go!"

Misty put her head in her hands.

"Flamethrower, Charizard!" But the giant Pokémon just stood there, yawning, "What's wrong with you? Battle, Charizard!"

"Tauros, Take Down!" commanded the trainer.

The Tauros came charging full force at Charizard. Just as it was about to slam into the Fire Pokémon, Charizard let out an enormous burst of flame that completely engulfed Tauros. The wild bull was scorched. Tauros was out!

Ash leaped into the air, cheering for his victory. But Charizard wasn't through. It took to the sky and began swooping down over the other diners in the restaurant, throwing flames in all directions.

Misty screamed, "Do something, Ash! Charizard is out of control!"

"Return!" Ash cried but it wouldn't listen. Tracey and Misty fell to the ground and covered their heads.

"Go, Poké Ball!" Prima's voice sailed up over the chaos as Slowbro, a big pink Pokémon appeared.

Ash stared in disbelief. What could a slow, sleepy Pokémon like Slowbro do against a raging Charizard?

"Disable!" Prima ordered. Slowbro shot a ray of light at the dive-bombing Charizard. Charizard froze in place.

"Okay, Slowbro," Prima said sweetly, "bring Charizard down just like that."

Slowbro floated the paralyzed Charizard

gently to the ground. Ash called Charizard back to its Poké Ball.

"I was sure I'd be able to handle it this time," Ash said sheepishly.

"A Pokémon trainer is only as good as his Pokémon," Prima said.

Ash defended himself. "I know that much!"

"I'm not sure you do," she said. "Once your Pokémon feel you care about them, they'll want to stand by you. But if you get too proud, they'll disobey you. You have to listen to your heart and connect with your Pokémon."

Ash stared at Prima, suddenly feeling ashamed.

"A Pokémon battle is never something for a trainer to do alone."

"I've earned all these badges," Ash sputtered. "Doesn't that count for anything?"

"Don't treat them so lightly, Ash. Your Pokémon fought hard to earn those for you. They're gifts that show how much your Pokémon care about you. And losing is a very important part of becoming a Pokémon Master."

"I don't get it," Ash said.

"You need to experience the pain and disappointment of defeat. It's easy to win — but when you lose you have to rely on your real strengths." Prima continued. "The people and the Pokémon you love and who love you back. If you want to compete in the Orange League, you have to become closer to your Pokémon than ever by battling side by side. As time goes on, you'll learn almost as much about your Pokémon as you do about yourself."

Ash stared at the ground. He knew Prima was right.

"You must continue your journey now," Prima said.

Ash nodded.

"Remember," she said softly, "no matter what happens, you can learn from it."

Ash didn't say a word for a long time after they left Prima. He rode silently next to his friends on Lapras's back. He was halfway to his goal of competing in the Orange League. But after meeting Prima, he suddenly felt like he was just a beginner. He had a lot to think about. One thing was clear though. He still wanted to win the Orange League Trophy, but now he wanted to win it for his Pokémon!

He was lost in thought when a scream snapped him out of it. He looked up and realized for the first time that they were approaching an island.

"Help!" He heard the scream again.

"Where's it coming from?" he asked excitedly.

"There!" Misty shouted.

Misty pointed to the rough waters that surged around rock formations just offshore of the island. A little girl was caught in a whirlpool that was swirling around between the rocks. She was clinging to a snow-white Seel and it didn't look like she'd be able to stay afloat much longer!

9

Electabuzz Attack

"Staryu! Go!" Misty jumped into the water. Her star-shaped Pokémon whisked her away toward the little girl. Ash and Tracey gripped tightly to Lapras, following as fast as they could. Then the little girl disappeared beneath the water and so did Misty.

Ash's eyes scanned the water. Nothing. Suddenly, three heads and the point of a star popped to the surface; Misty and Staryu, the little girl and her Seel.

Lapras swung around so Ash and Tracey could pull them out of the water.

"Is everybody okay?" Ash asked.

"I think so," Misty said. She helped the little girl get settled. "Are you okay?"

"Yes," the little girl said, smiling at Misty, "thanks to you."

"Mahri!" A teenage boy was racing down to a dock, followed by a group of younger boys. Mahri waved to him.

"That's my brother, Rudy!" Mahri said excitedly. Lapras picked up speed, anxious to deliver the little girl safely back to land. She leaped into Rudy's arms the moment her feet hit the dock.

"Mahri! You had me so worried!" her brother cried.

"I'm sorry," said Mahri.

"Thank you so much," Rudy looked at Misty. "I can never repay you."

Misty blushed as Rudy kissed her hand. "I'm glad we were there," said Misty.

"So am I. I'm Rudy and this is Mahri," he said.

"I'm Misty, and these are my friends, Ash and Tracey," Misty smiled.

"Well, beautiful Misty and her friends,

allow me to give you a tour of the island."

Ash didn't quite understand what this Rudy character was doing. But he knew one thing: this mushy stuff had to stop.

"We'd love to," Ash interrupted, "but we're on our way to Trovita Island. I'm challenging the Gym Leader there to get my Spikeshell Badge."

Rudy smiled and said, "This is Trovita Island, and I am the Gym Leader."

Ash's jaw dropped. "Uhh — oh — then — I challenge you to a battle!"

Rudy nodded. "I accept."

Rudy walked to a motorboat on the dock and jumped in. "Follow me!" he said.

Lapras followed the motorboat along the shore. Soon they pulled up to a dock in front of a purplish stone building that had GYM carved above the door.

"So? Are we going to battle?" Ash trailed Rudy and Misty into the gym.

"Yes. Three rounds. One-on-one," Rudy said. "But first I want to show you my Pokémon."

"What's up with this guy?" Ash asked Tracey.

"Beats me," Tracey replied.

"The days of simply teaching Pokémon attacks are over," Rudy said as he held open the doors for everyone. "You can actually improve their abilities by training them in something completely unrelated."

Ash was stopped in his tracks by the unbelievable scene in the gym. Music was blasting and dozens of Pokémon were dancing! An Electabuzz in sweatpants was doing

the twist. A Hitmonchan bounced around in a little workout skirt. An Exeggutor jumped up and down doing a kind of jitterbug. In the corner, a group of Rattata were line dancing.

"Dancing?" Misty sputtered.

"We teach dance to all the Pokémon. It really improves their moves," Rudy said.

"That's so smart," Misty said, beaming at Rudy. "You're amazing!"

"All right!" Ash couldn't stand it anymore. "Let's get on with it. Let's battle!"

Ash and Rudy stood on either side of a playing field set atop the plateau of an enormous rock formation. There were hundred-foot dropoffs in every direction that fell directly to the water. The field sat so close to these edges, in fact, that spectators had to watch from a hot air balloon.

"First, an Electric Pokémon battle!" Rudy announced.

"Go for it, Pikachu!" Pikachu gave Ash a confident nod.

"I can't wait to see your Pokémon dance!" Misty shouted from the balloon.

Rudy waved at her. Ash stared in

disbelief. Who was she rooting for anyway?

"Electabuzz! I'm counting on you!" Rudy shouted.

Electabuzz appeared, doing a little jig as a warmup.

"Pikachu! Thunderbolt!" Pikachu summoned up its power and let out a blast of electricity that lit up the field. But Electabuzz had no reaction.

"Electric Attacks won't work," Tracey said, sketching the view from above.

"It's okay, Pikachu, we'll use normal attacks," Ash said. "Quick Attack! Now!"

Pikachu darted quickly down the field, showing off its agility. But Electabuzz was ready. It quickly blocked Pikachu's path. Pikachu slammed into Electabuzz and was sent flying backward.

"Pikachu!" Ash cried, hoping his little yellow friend would pull itself upright.

"Electabuzz! Thunder Punch!" Rudy shouted.

Pikachu had no time to recover. Electabuzz slammed into it with heavy force. Pikachu went spinning backward, almost to the edge of the plateau.

"Pikachu!" Ash flung himself toward Pikachu and grabbed it just in time.

"This match is over!" Rudy announced. "Round one goes to Electabuzz."

"It's okay, Pikachu." Ash was more concerned about his Pokémon right now. "Take a rest. Are you okay?"

Before Pikachu could respond, Ash heard Misty's voice. "That was amazing, Rudy!"

He looked up and Misty was waving at his opponent. She was smiling and cheering like she wanted him to win!

10

Squirtle vs. the Dancing Pokémon

Ash tried to stay focused on the match. He couldn't worry about Misty right now. He had a badge to win!

"Bulbasaur! I choose you!" he said victoriously.

"Exeggutor, do your stuff," commanded Rudy confidently.

A three-headed Pokémon appeared on the field. Exeggutor had long green palms coming out of its three heads and a brown body that looked like the trunk of a palm tree.

"Start the music!" Rudy shouted.

The air filled with music and Exeggutor started dancing down the whole field. It swayed back and forth, closing in on Bulbasaur.

Ash refused to be distracted. "Bulbasaur! Razor Leaf!"

The sky filled with green blades slicing through the air.

"Exeggutor, Dancing Attack!" Rudy yelled.

The three-headed Pokémon dodged every leaf, dancing its way through an impossible obstacle course!

"Again, Bulbasaur! Razor Leaf!" Ash commanded

It was no use. Exeggutor danced its way out of any trouble.

"Egg Bomb!" Rudy demanded.

Exeggutor stopped and launched a huge white egg straight at Bulbasaur. The egg crashed into Bulbasaur and nearly knocked it out.

"Come on, Bulbasaur!" Ash tried to focus. He had to win this round. "Sleep Powder!"

Bulbasaur's bulb spewed a white mist. It rained down on Exeggutor. The Pokémon's eyes, all six of them, began to close. Half asleep, it continued to sway back and forth across the field straight toward the edge. Exeggutor was about to fall off the cliff!

"Oh, no!" Ash cried. He didn't want to win this way. "Bulbasaur, use your Vine Whip!"

Bulbasaur came to the rescue. The Grass Pokémon threw its vines over the edge. In one swift move, it caught Exeggutor and reeled it back. Ash could hear Rudy sigh with relief.

"I appreciate your helping my Pokémon," he said. He pulled Exeggutor back to its Poké Ball. "But it doesn't mean I'll go easy on you. We're tied and this is the final round! The

third battle is for Water Types. I dedicate this victory to Misty with many thanks for saving my sister. Starmie! Come out!"

Ash looked up at Misty. She smiled and waved down to Rudy.

Who's she rooting for anyway? Ash wondered.

He had to concentrate. Which Pokémon? He had to remind himself it was a Water challenge.

"Squirtle! I choose you!" Ash declared. Squirtle charged out of its Poké Ball.

"Starmie! End this now! Water Gun!" Rudy began the battle.

"Squirtle! Water Gun!" Ash countered.

The two Pokémon leaped up and blasted each other with powerful torrents of water.

"Okay," Rudy said, "let's dance!"

Again, Rudy's Pokémon avoided attacks with its dancing skills. Squirtle's blasts were useless. Ash didn't know what to do. He needed help.

Starmie started to spin faster and faster. A glow radiated all around it. It was creating a big electric field.

"That Starmie can use Electric Attacks!" Tracey said, shocked. "Squirtle's weak against electric attacks. This isn't good."

Ash watched helplessly as Starmie built up more and more power. He knew Squirtle had no defense. He could see the Spikeshell Badge slipping through his fingers. Ash had never before felt so defeated in the middle of a battle.

"Ash!" The sound sent a jolt through Ash's system. He looked up at the balloon. Misty was leaning over the side of the basket.

"What are you doing?! Pull yourself together Ash!!" she yelled.

Ash felt a surge of energy. She was yelling at him. He should have been mad, but for some reason, it made him feel great.

"A trainer is the only one who can bring out his Pokémon's power!" she cried.

"I know that!" Ash shouted back.

"Then do something!" Misty shouted. "This is no time to be awestruck by the dance."

Ash kicked into action. "Squirtle! Aim your Water Gun at the ground!" A new authority filled his voice. He was ready to win!

Squirtle blew a fierce blast of water downward. When the blast hit the ground, it catapulted Squirtle into the sky. Not only did Squirtle avoid Starmie's electrical blast but it could now hit Starmie from above.

But Squirtle had catapulted too far. It was soaring past the edge of the cliff. Squirtle was going to plunge hundreds of feet to the ocean below!

"Squirtle!" Ash cried.

Squirtle tucked itself into its shell and began to spin. Water fanned out from openings in its shell. It turned itself into a kind of propeller.

"I can't believe it," Misty gasped. "Squirtle just learned Hydro Pump!"

The Pokémon had learned a new attack

84

just in time to save itself. The force of the Hydro Pump brought Squirtle back up to the cliff and onto the playing field.

"All right!" shouted Ash. "Hydro Pump!"

"Pika!" Pikachu cheered.

Starmie stood centerfield, ready to attack.

"Squirtle! Skull Bash!"

The pumped-up Squirtle bashed into Starmie, hurling it into the air.

"Starmie!" Rudy cried. It was too late. Starmie fell to the ground and fainted.

It was all over. The match was decided. Ash had won!

"Way to go, Ash!"

"Yeah!"

Ash could hear his friends yelling from above. It felt great. He held Squirtle high in the air, jumping up and down for joy.

"I lost to you, Ash." Rudy seemed amazed. But he held out his hand. "The Spikeshell Badge is yours."

Ash looked at the badge in his palm. It was a beautiful star-shaped seashell badge with a kind of gold glow. He took it and looked up to the balloon. Then he held his new badge up in the air for his friends to see.

"I won the Spikeshell Badge!" he bellowed, and it seemed like he was loud enough for the whole world to hear!

11

Friends

"Can you believe it?" Ash hadn't stopped talking since the competition. "Only one more badge and I can compete in the Orange League!"

They were packing up Lapras, preparing to head out in search of the fourth seashell badge.

Misty sighed. "Yes, Ash, we heard you the first ten times. Let's go," she said.

"I was pretty good, wasn't I?" Ash asked as they made their way out to the open ocean.

"Yeah, you were good," Misty admitted. "But there's always room for improvement."

"Well, it might have helped if you hadn't rooted for my opponent!" Ash said.

"Ash Ketchum! I was not rooting for your opponent," Misty protested. "I was simply admiring his inventive form of training." She stopped talking and stared out at a beautiful sunset that was just beginning.

"Sorry, Ash," Misty said unexpectedly. "I'll always root for you. We're friends."

Ash smiled and looked away.

"Whatever," he said casually, but he felt great. It was great to have friends to depend on. Lorelei's words floated through his head:

"You never win by your own power alone. You always need the help of your friends."

Ash stole a quick look at his friends: Misty and Tracey, Pikachu, Togepi, and Lapras. He looked at the collection of Poké Balls hooked on his belt; Bulbasaur, Charizard, Squirtle, and the rest.

Finally, he looked out toward the horizon. Beautiful colors were spreading across the sky.

He would do it! He felt absolutely sure. He would win the fourth badge and get the chance to compete in the Orange League. Not because he was a great Pokémon trainer — which, of course, he was.

No. He'd win because he had friends. Great friends, both human and Pokémon!